WORLD DISASTERS!

VOLCANO

BRIAN KNAPP

STECK-VAUGHN
L I B R A R Y

Austin, Texas

Published in the United States in 1990 by Steck-Vaughn Co., Austin, Texas, a subsidiary of National Education Corporation.

© Earthscape Editions 1989
© Macmillan Publishers Limited 1989

First published in 1989
by Macmillan Children's Books
A division of Macmillan Publishers Ltd

Designed and produced by Earthscape Editions,
Sonning Common, Oxon, England

Cover design by Julian Holland

Illustrations by
Duncan McCrae and Tim Smith

Printed and bound in the United States.

1 2 3 4 5 6 7 8 9 0 LB 94 93 92 91 90

Photographic credits

t = top b = bottom l = left r = right

All photographs are from the Earthscape Editions photographic library except for the following: title page Austin Post/USGS; 9bl, 11b, 13bl, 22bl Stephen Porter; 9tr, 10, 11t Keith Ronnholm; 15t, 33br C.M. Clapperton; 34 Japan National Tourist Organization; 15b, 32, 40br Popperfoto; 16, 17t, 27, 33tl ZEFA; 17b Frank Lane Agency; 20, 21t, 21b Colorific; 24/25 British Museum (Natural History)/L. B. Sanderson; 29 British Museum (Natural History); 30, 31t A. Gonzalez/Reflex; 31b P. Cavendish/Reflex; 37 G. Wadge/NERC.

cover: Matthew Shipp/Science Photo Library
Krafla Volcano, near Lake Myvatn, North Iceland

Library of Congress Cataloging-in-Publication Data

Knapp, Brian J.
    Volcano/Brian Knapp.
        p.   cm. — (World disasters)
    Includes index.
    Summary: Discusses how and why volcanoes erupt, what effect these disasters have on the earth, and how some of the world's great volcanoes eruptions occurred.
    ISBN 0-8114-2373-5
    1. Volcanoes—Juvenile literature.   2. Natural disasters—Juvenile   literature. [1. Volcanoes]   I. Title.
II. Series: World disasters! (Austin, Tex)
QE521.3K53 1989
551.2'1—dc20   89-11584
                                                              CIP
                                                              AC

Note to the reader
In this book there are some words in the text that are printed in **bold** type. This shows that the word is listed in the glossary on page 46. The glossary gives a brief explanation of words that may be new to you.

Contents

Introduction

In this book we will look at some of the world's great volcanic **disasters** and how people have learned to live with **volcanoes**. To understand why volcanic disasters happen and how to be prepared for **eruptions** we have to know first a little about the part played by volcanoes in the history of the Earth.

Inside the Earth

The Earth is made up of many different materials arranged in layers inside one another. The pattern is similar to the layers of an onion. The outer layer is the solid rock called the **crust**. It forms the continents, ocean floors, mountains, and valleys of the Earth's surface. It makes the land on which we live and the land beneath the oceans.

Underneath the crust is another layer of material called the **mantle** and inside this is the **core**.

The Earth's rock layers contain many **radioactive** materials. These radioactive materials release a great deal of heat, similar to the way electrical power is generated in a nuclear power station. However, heat generated within the Earth cannot easily escape. Instead it builds up. Over the four and a half billion years since the Earth was formed, the heat produced by the radioactive materials has caused some of the inner layers to melt. The upper part of the mantle is one of these liquid regions. As a result the crust of the Earth floats on this liquid rock like a log floating on a pond.

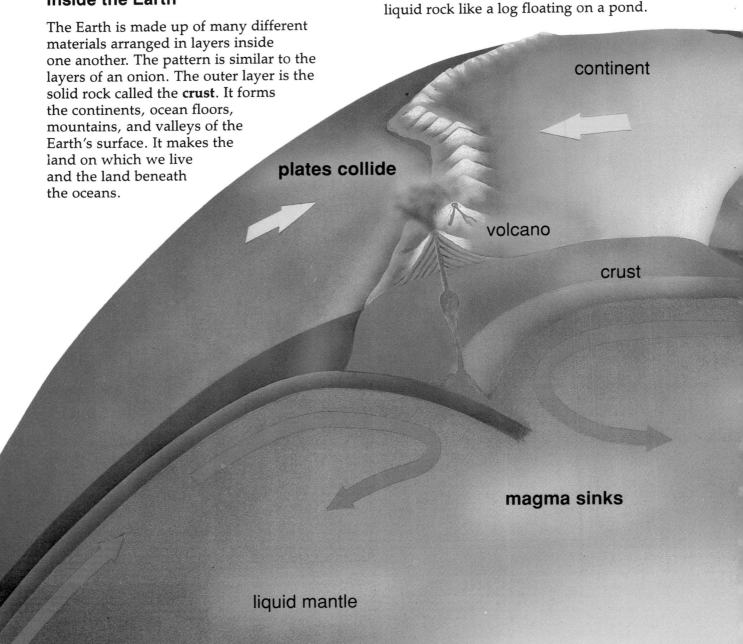

continent

plates collide

volcano

crust

magma sinks

liquid mantle

We call molten material fresh from the mantle **magma**. It is the molten rock from the mantle that sometimes comes to the surface as volcanoes.

How volcanoes occur

For thousands of millions of years of the Earth's history, the liquid mantle has been churning over. The movement of molten rock is similar to the way water turns over when it is heated and boils in a saucepan.
This process is called **convection**.
As it churns, the mantle drags against the underside of the solid and brittle crust.

▼ *This diagram shows how the Earth is made up of crust, mantle, and core. The Earth's surface crust has been exaggerated in thickness to make the diagram clear. However, the crust is really just a thin skin and is easily dragged along by the moving mantle.*

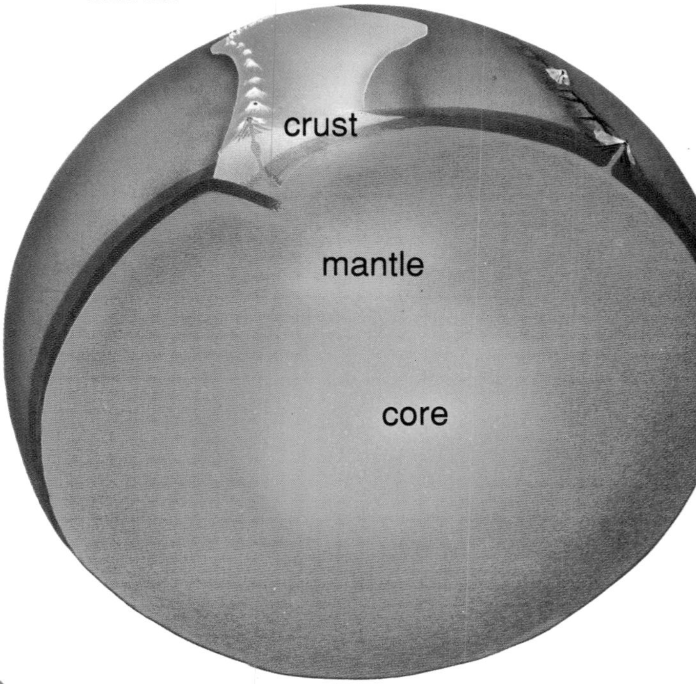

crust

mantle

core

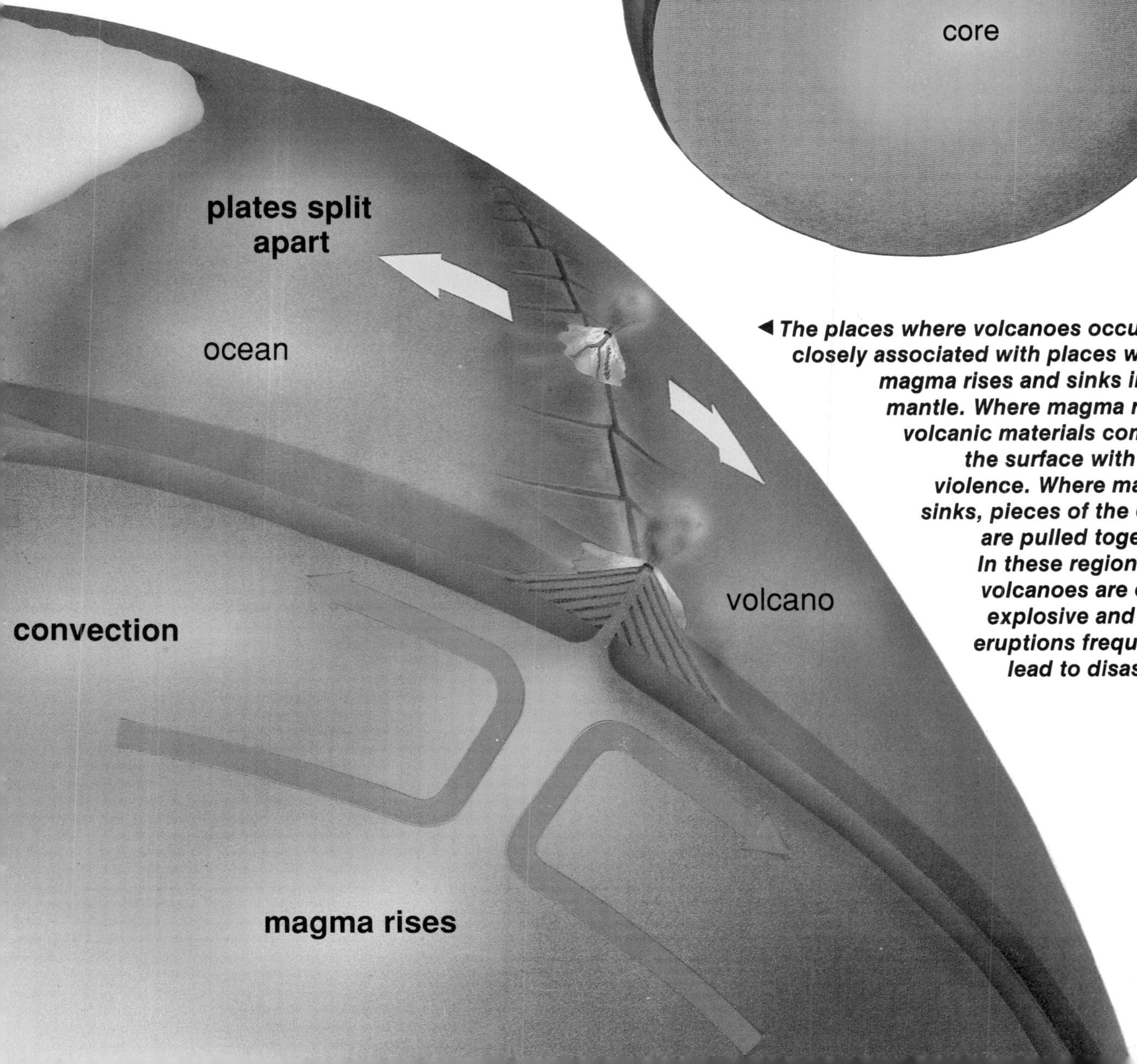

plates split apart

ocean

convection

volcano

magma rises

◄ *The places where volcanoes occur are closely associated with places where magma rises and sinks in the mantle. Where magma rises, volcanic materials come to the surface with little violence. Where magma sinks, pieces of the crust are pulled together. In these regions the volcanoes are often explosive and their eruptions frequently lead to disasters.*

At the present time the crust is broken into over a dozen large pieces. Each piece is called a crustal **plate**. The splitting has made the Earth's surface resemble a giant eggshell that has just been cracked with a spoon.

Convection is still at work in the mantle. In some places it drags plates apart, causing great cracks to open in the crust. Where plates split, the magma easily flows to the surface as rivers and fountains of **lava**.

Because magma can flow up these splits easily the volcanoes produced this way are not very dangerous and they rarely have large explosions. Nevertheless, lava flows can still cause disasters for those who live near them.

Repeated eruptions of magma have also gradually piled huge amounts of lava on the ocean floors. A few of these undersea volcanoes have even risen above the ocean surface and form some of the largest mountains on Earth. These types of volcano are mostly found on mid-ocean islands, such as Iceland (in the Atlantic Ocean) or Hawaii (in the Pacific Ocean).

Where two plates collide many large **earthquakes** and violent volcanoes are produced. In these places magma has melted its way through the crust up a **vent**. This vent concentrates all the energy and often causes an explosive start to an eruption. These violent explosive volcanoes cause most of the world's volcanic disasters. Some famous explosive volcanoes are Mount Etna and Mount Vesuvius in Italy, Mount St. Helens in the United States, and Nevado del Ruiz in Columbia.

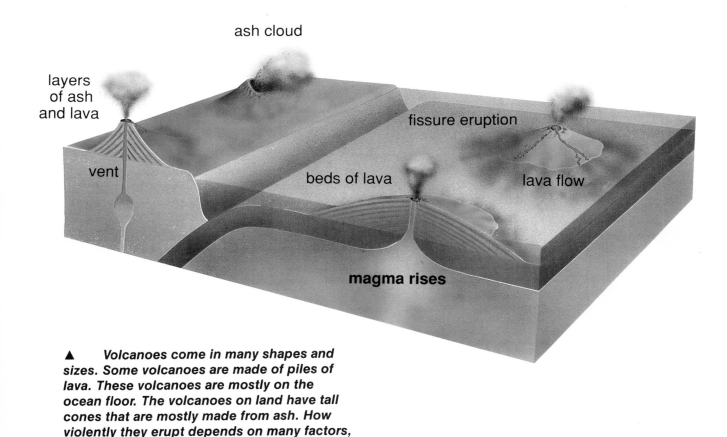

ash cloud

layers of ash and lava

vent

fissure eruption

beds of lava

lava flow

magma rises

▲ *Volcanoes come in many shapes and sizes. Some volcanoes are made of piles of lava. These volcanoes are mostly on the ocean floor. The volcanoes on land have tall cones that are mostly made from ash. How violently they erupt depends on many factors, including the time since the last eruption and the chemicals in the magma.*

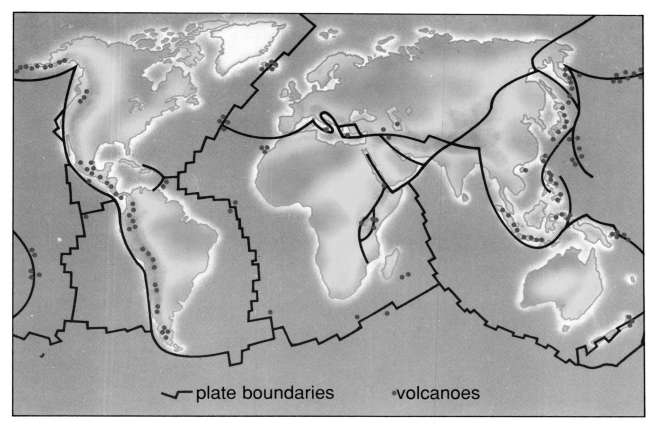

plate boundaries · volcanoes

▲ *This map of the world shows the main plates. Some of their boundaries run down the centers of oceans, while others are close to the edges of the continents. Volcanoes occur at the cracked edges of plates.*

Volcanic materials

Volcanoes and the **volcanic materials** they produce vary widely. In some cases the volcano explodes and magma is blown out of the central pipe or vent. These very fine pieces of magma are called **ash**. Sometimes magma flows out of the vent or out of a split in the ground just like water. This liquid material is called lava. Volcanoes also send out large amounts of hot poisonous gases and steam. These make up the giant clouds that form above an erupting volcano.

As ash flies out of a vent it can get carried by the wind and cover very large areas. The hot gases can move over the nearby land at speeds greater than an express train. The rivers of lava can flow faster than water flooding down a river. These make the area around erupting volcanoes dangerous for people and wildlife.

Where volcanoes occur

Magma nearly always rises to the surface at the edges of the plates. This means that volcanoes are mostly spaced out around the Earth in long thin lines. One string of very large mountains stretches down the middle of the Atlantic Ocean. Iceland is the tip of one of these mountains. This great mountain chain, larger than any mountain chain on land, is called the Mid-Atlantic Ridge. Another plate edge stretches all the way around the Pacific Ocean. This is a place where plates collide. It contains many explosive volcanoes. Because of this it is called the Pacific Ring of Fire.

Not much of the Earth's surface is affected by volcanoes, so most people are safe from violent volcanic eruptions. However, in 1980 one violent volcanic eruption was witnessed by hundreds of millions of people on their television screens. The story of the eruption of this volcano, called Mount St. Helens, and the disaster it brought to local people, forms the next part of the book.

Explosion

The story of Mount St. Helens tells of the devastating power of a volcanic eruption. It clearly shows how difficult it is for scientists to forecast what will happen and when it will happen. People who live near the edges of the Earth's plates may be at risk from volcanic eruptions.

Mount St. Helens awakes

Mount St. Helens is a spectacular peak in the Cascade Mountains of Washington in the northwest United States. The mountain had been rumbling for months before the final eruption. Puffs of steam and ash had already come from the vent of the volcano. The people who came to visit the beautiful scenery of Mount St. Helens during the spring of 1980 found it difficult to believe the mountain they saw was really only a delicate "cap" of rock and ice which could explode at any moment.

Mount St. Helens that year was like a soda bottle that has been shaken and is waiting to explode as the cap is released. The scientists who kept recording changes on the mountain had expected the volcano to explode upward. Nobody thought a **landslide** would allow the boiling gases and ash to burst out sideways.

ash cloud blown toward Yakima

blast area where trees were knocked down

Mount St. Helens

forest

mudflows in Toutle River

▲ *Mount St. Helens is part of the Cascade mountain chain. The mountain is surrounded by hills and valleys. The ash and gases were stopped from spreading out farther by a hill ridge. The rivers of mud were forced to follow the deep river valleys. In this way the shape of the landscape restricted the disaster area.*

0

miles

50

▼ ► These two photographs of Mount St. Helens show how the perfect volcano cone was ripped apart during the explosion. The top was simply blown away and a gaping hole was left in the summit.

The scientists could not predict the stupendous way in which the mountain would literally tear itself apart on the morning of Thursday, May 18, 1980. The eruption cost 63 lives and destroyed 212 square miles of surrounding land.

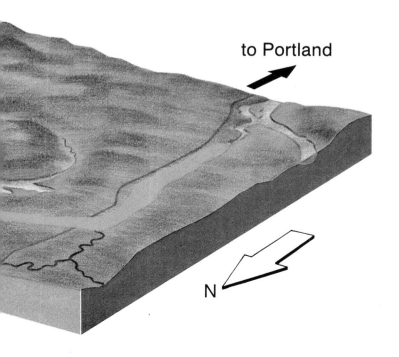

to Portland

N

The eruption

"Oh, dear God, . . . I just can't describe this—it's pitch black. This is hell on Earth I'm walking through. One step at a time. If I can just keep walking."

The man who said this was a journalist, David Crockett, who had gone to film the Mount St. Helen's eruption. He just didn't expect to find himself engulfed within seconds by the suffocating, swirling ash that poured from the volcano. David Crockett was rescued after nine terrifying hours of stumbling through the dark on the mountainside.

Keith Ronnholm, the scientist who obtained the photographs of the start of the explosion, was several miles away from the mountain when the eruption occurred. At first he was amazed by the scene that enfolded in front of him. Then, as the gas cloud rushed toward him, he realized his life was in danger. He raced away in his truck, driving recklessly at great speed. He was trying to escape from the volcanic gas and ash that were sweeping down the mountainside. Others, who could not drive as fast, were less lucky. Several families died in their cars, suffocated by the gas and ash.

The burning cloud

As the ash and gas swept across the landscape they burned and destroyed everything. On the slopes of the mountain, trees were simply uprooted and carried away. A few miles from the volcano fully grown trees almost 22 feet high were pushed over like matchsticks and laid out in neat rows against the hillsides. Even forests up to 20 miles from the mountain were affected. Each was cleanly stripped of its branches. The gas and ash cloud killed countless mammals, birds, fish, and insects. Within seconds it had turned a beautiful forest into a wasteland.

The floods that followed

The glacier that covered the top of Mount St. Helens melted into rivers of water and clouds of steam when the volcano erupted. Rivers quickly became swollen by the melting ice. Within a few hours there were **floods** of water and mud over a wide area. Logs, trucks, bridges, and even houses were swept away.

The ash cloud

The cloud, drifting with the wind, soon lost its poisonous gases, and the small fragments of ash cooled considerably. As the cloud drifted east it reached Yakima, the nearest town downwind of Mount St. Helens. The ash that fell from the cloud covered the town in a gray coating that looked like dirty snow. The ash got into everything, forcing people indoors. It got into car engines bringing them to a halt. It got under doors and between window frames. In Yakima the world seemed about to end . . .

▼ *This was the scene seconds after the explosion began.*

The next few days

Television viewers were unaware of the horror that befell the people who were still close to the volcano. Commentators on the local radio station even made jokes about it. One disc jockey commented on the ash cloud that was drifting eastward across the United States, carried by the wind:
"If you were thinking of coming on vacation to Washington this summer, don't bother. This year Washington is coming to visit you!"

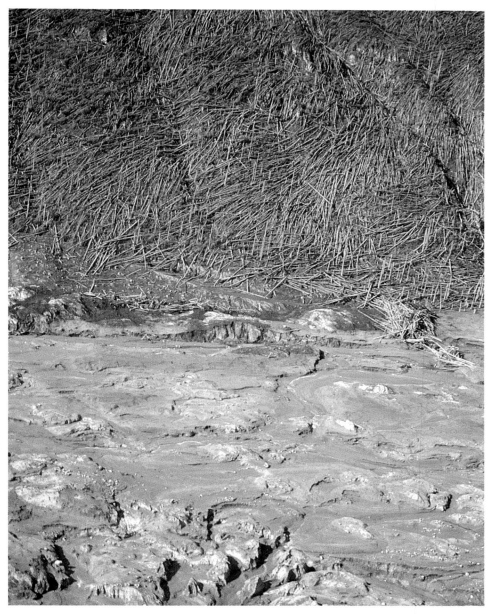

▲　The ash cloud turned day into night at Yakima, a small town to the east of Mount St. Helens. Many days were spent cleaning up the streets of Yakima before the town could be made fit for living again.

◄　The burning gas and ash cloud flattened trees near the mountain and left them laid out on the ground like matchsticks. In front the land has been masked with the remains of the mudflow that swept along the Toutle River Valley.

The result

After the initial explosion the eruption continued for four whole days, discharging millions of tons of ash and gas. By the fourth day the mountain was visible from behind the cloud of gases which had previously hidden the summit. Then it became clear that the top 1,300 feet of the mountain had been blown away. In its place there was a vast horseshoe-shaped **crater** over 1¼ miles across. Mount St. Helens had thrown nearly 7,000 million tons of material over the nearby land, adding to the landscape enough volume of rock to fill every skyscraper in New York City, over 30 times.

Clearing up

In the town of Yakima the 51,000 residents began the long process of clearing up the 600,000 tons of ash that had fallen on their houses, on their streets, and in their gardens. The residents had to scrape ash from their roofs before its weight caused any collapse. They had to shake all their fruit trees to remove the ash so that the flowers could be pollinated. Farmers tried to do the same for the crops in the field. The governor of Washington had already declared an emergency so extra relief funds could be used to help pay for the cleanup.

The flooded rivers had carried all kinds of **debris** with them, which piled up in the lower stretches of the rivers. Portland harbor was blocked by the debris. Workers quickly began to remove it, so that the harbor could be used again.

The tourists

Over the next month there were four more small eruptions. Even after the eruptions stopped there was still a real danger of further explosions. Therefore, for the first few months the authorities kept all the access roads to the area closed. Gradually it became clear that the worst of the danger was past, and there was pressure to open

▼ *Mount St. Helens as it appears today. The misty shape of the mountain can be seen through the scorched trees. These trees lie at the edge of the area devastated by the eruption, so you can see just how large the devastation zone was.*

the area to the thousands of tourists who wanted to visit the site. The local people were also eager to let the tourists in. They could earn money from the tourist trade which would help them get back some of the money they had lost in the disaster.

Within a couple of years or so the federal government had built a new access road so that tourists could come and see the spectacular damage. The government thought this was particularly important as it would educate people about the dangers from eruptions.

Getting back to normal

Gradually life got back to normal in the towns surrounding the volcano. People began to log some of the trees that were knocked down, others started to farm again, and many more are now working in the tourist trade. The forest service started trying to make the **vegetation** grow on the bare volcano slopes before rainstorms could wash away the fragile exposed topsoil. The cost was high: it is thought that $600 million had to be paid out in insurance claims, relief, and repairs. It could have been worse. The eruption was small on a world scale.

▲   *The Mount St. Helens area has now been protected as a National Monument for the benefit of future generations.*

▼   *Flooding was a major problem for people many miles away from the volcano.*

▼   *Tourists gather around a car destroyed during the eruption.*

Tongues of Fire

One of the most common types of volcanic material is molten rock called lava. As lava flows out of a volcano it is extremely hot. It is always over 1,470°F and sometimes over 2,100°F, the temperature of white-hot steel.

Lava flowing across the surface of the land can be one of the most spectacular sights in the natural world. At night the tongues of yellow, orange, and red lava flecked with black floating pieces of solid rock light up the sky. When the lava flows like a river over the edge of a cliff it turns into a fantastic fiery waterfall. If it flows over flat land it spreads out to make a boiling colorful lake.

Floods of lava

What is spectacularly beautiful when seen from a place of safety can spell death and destruction to those trapped in its path.

Fortunately really large floods of lava are rare. No one has seen such an event in recorded history. **Geologists** know that large lava floods happened in the past, by studying the rocks in the landscape. Floods of lava have moved at hundreds of miles an hour and over thousands of square miles. Huge parts of the United States and India are covered with rocks made from floods of lava. If such a flood occurred in our lifetimes it would probably be the biggest ever natural disaster.

▼ *Rivers and fountains of molten lava look very dramatic. The example shown here is from Iceland, where the lava is very runny. In this photograph lava gushes along a long crack in the land and then flows toward the distant sea. It is typical of places where crustal plates are pulling apart.*

Lava flows that occur in regions where crustal plates meet are much more sticky. As a result lava flows are much thicker and move more slowly. However, people with homes and land near either kind of moving lava flows see how dangerous and destructive they really are.

Danger from lava

Lava flows on a smaller scale are much more common. Some volcanoes produce lava flows almost every day. Mostly they do not get very far and often the end of a lava flow moves so slowly you can walk out of its path. When the lava cools, and it is broken down by the effects of rain, it often forms a **fertile soil**. Therefore people farm the land closer and closer to volcanoes, putting their property and sometimes themselves at risk from the tongues of fire.

Mount Etna

The people of Sicily are some of those who have been most at risk in the past. They have built their homes farther and farther up the slopes of Mount Etna. Here the soil is fertile, whereas the rest of the land is poor for crops. The farmers can grow grains, grapes, and other fruits on the volcano's slopes. But every time Mount Etna erupts, some of the people suffer. The last time there was an eruption, people went toward the tongue of lava that was pushing its way down the mountainside. They placed a statue of their patron saint in front of the lava and prayed,

"Dear Saint, we pray to you to save our village, to stop the terrifying wall of molten rock from burning our vineyards, burying our land, and destroying our homes." However, the lava flow did not stop and many homes and vineyards were destroyed. It will take decades for the new lava to break down into good soil again. In the meantime, farmers have been forced to seek work in towns so they could feed their families. However, farm work is not good training for town jobs, and many farmers simply had to join the people who are unemployed.

▲ Some volcanoes erupt regularly and send lava flows streaming down their flanks. Buildings in the path of lava flows stand little chance of survival.

◄ A lava flow crushes and burns vineyards near the village of Foruazzo on the slopes of Mount Etna. The farmers are powerless to stop the destruction.

Rivers of lava

In Iceland, in southern Italy, and on Hawaii, rivers of lava are produced during eruptions every few years. Usually lava flows come to a halt before they cause too much damage. As they flow over the landscape they cool and change from a runny to a sticky liquid. Then a rock crust called **pumice** forms on top of the lava flow. Gradually the end of the lava flow cools, the rock crust hardens, and the lava stops. However, sometimes lava flows do not stop before they reach people's homes. This is what happened on Heimaey, a small island off the coast of Iceland.

▼ Snow falling on the island of Heimaey helped to show the size of the lava flow as it advanced across the harbor. The hot lava caused great clouds of steam to rise from the surface of the sea.

Heimaey

Iceland depends greatly on its fishing industry, and a sheltered harbor is of great benefit during winter storms. Heimaey is important to the people of Iceland because it has such a harbor. By 1973 there were over 1,000 homes on Heimaey and the population had grown to over 5,000 people. The fishing industry had made them some of the most prosperous people in Iceland.

In January 1973 the volcano Helgafell erupted close to the harbor on Heimaey. Because Icelanders know the dangers of volcanoes well, everyone on the island was **evacuated** within four hours of the start of the eruption. People left their houses and all their belongings and escaped by boat.

Lava fountains spurted up from the slopes of Helgafell and quickly built a new volcanic **cone**. It was named Kirkefell. The

flow of lava from Kirkefell seemed unstoppable and soon threatened the town and its inhabitants.

In the first few hours the volcano lobbed fiery lumps of lava high in the air. When they landed on houses, the wooden structures were immediately burned out. Then the lava advanced in several directions at once. One arm lunged toward the edge of the town of Heimaey, its wall of crusted lava crushing houses in its path. Almost more important was the surge of lava that threatened to block off the entrance to the harbor. As the lava advanced and the entrance narrowed the water trapped inside almost reached the boiling point.

Although no lives were lost, this event was a disaster to the people of Iceland because the harbor was so important to the fishing fleet. Taxes had to be raised nationwide to help raise the money to pay for the damage and loss of trade.

▲   *Because there was little wind during the period of the eruption, the ash fell back near the volcano and started to bury the town.*

▼   *As lava advanced toward the town, the houses on the outskirts were buried. Nobody could stop them being crushed and burned.*

Rivers of Destruction

Some volcanoes are tall, majestic mountains. Many have snow and ice on their summits. When an eruption occurs, the snow and ice are melted and vast amounts of water pour down the sides of the mountain. This water gathers into rivers, swelling them so much that they tear at their banks and often spill out from their channels. The ground becomes full of water and soon there are landslides everywhere. These push more and more mud and rock into the rivers until the water is like liquid cement.

Rivers of mud

People who lived near Mount St. Helens now know rivers full of mud and rock are powerful and destructive. These rivers can knock down buildings, smash houses, and overturn cars. Nothing can stand in these rivers' ways. Bridges and roads just disappear. People in parts of the world that are at risk know and dread this sequence of events. The people of the Indonesian island of Java even have a special word that is now used to describe all volcanic **mudflows**. They call them **lahars**.

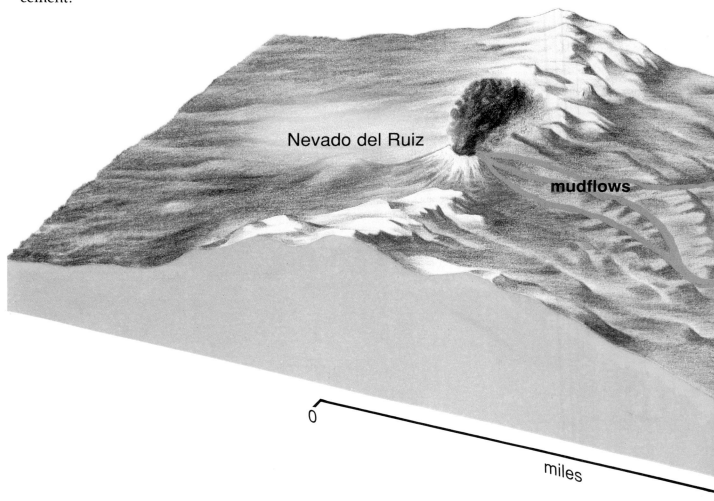

▲ *This landscape diagram shows how the Armero disaster happened.*

Disaster in a valley

In the mountains fertile land is scarce and is often found only in the bottoms of valleys. People rely on the land for their livelihood and thus they must live in the valley bottom. People also have to live near rivers to get water. Many villages are therefore not just in the valley bottom, but also near the river. This is the very place where danger from a mudflow or a flood is worst.

In 1985 a volcano about 19,500 feet high, called Nevado del Ruiz, erupted in an uninhabited part of Columbia.

It is one of many volcanoes that make up the high South American mountain range called the Andes.

▲ *The upper slopes of many volcanoes are covered with thick ice and snow. The picture shows that heat from the volcano has melted the ice from the summit. Armero's fate was sealed when Nevado del Ruiz exploded and melted the summit ice.*

Although Nevado del Ruiz produced a large amount of ash there was little immediate damage. But as some of the snow and ice on the mountain melted it was to cause one of the biggest mudflows in history.

In a valley over 30 miles from Nevado del Ruiz lies the town of Armero. It is famous for its crops of rice, cotton, and coffee. Only one part of the town occupies higher ground in the valley floor. The rest sprawls over the river **floodplain**. Its small river, known as the La Lagunilla, gathers its waters from the flanks of Nevado del Ruiz.

One night the waters that filled the head of the valley were to spell death and destruction to all those who lived on the low land, to almost all the town's 23,000 people. It began with the volcano's eruption.

La Lagunilla River

Armero

N

50

The eruption begins

The eruption began in the late afternoon. The volcano blew ash 26,000 feet into the air. Brown ash started falling from the sky onto Armero like snow, but it was hard and gritty. An hour later it started raining. The radio station told people to stay calm. Very few left their homes.

Imagine the scene as a little girl named Esmeralda slept in a small room in the town. All was quiet and peaceful. It was 11 p.m. Then something disturbed the peace. She heard a sound like the wind rustling in the trees. A dog howled, pigs began to squeal, geese began to honk. There was something wrong. The rustling grew louder and changed to a dull crashing sound. Then a wall of mud burst in to the ground floor of the house, tearing at the brickwork and gushing up the stairs where the family were huddled together in fright. There was no warning of the advance of the mudflow. Miraculously their house survived and they were able to get to the roof to await rescue. Unfortunately 20,000 other people in the town were buried by the seething mud and water. Armero disappeared in about 15 minutes.

▼ **Armero was built close to the bottom of a river valley. Here you see that only houses on slightly higher ground escaped. The rest of the town was washed away by the mudflow.**

◀ *The photograph shows how survivors had to stand on their rooftops and wait patiently until helicopters were able to take them to safety. The people in this picture were lucky. In the background you can see that the houses have been completely destroyed.*

Why few people escaped

When people flew over the scene of the disaster the next morning little could be seen of the town. About 85 percent of Armero had been destroyed. One pilot said, "It looked like a beach at low tide, just mud and driftwood. Trees, houses, and cars were all carried off."

The eruption of a volcano is not like the approach of a storm. It cannot be tracked, so people cannot be warned easily. There had been some earth **tremors** a few months before and a few puffs of smoke had come from the volcano. Nevado del Ruiz had not erupted for 400 years. No one in Armero believed it would erupt again. Who was going to leave their homes, crops, and land, "just in case"? The radio advised people to stay calm. Families in Armero thought they were so far away from the volcano that they would be safe.

▶ *The man in the photograph was one of the first to be rescued. He is still covered with mud. Helicopters were the only way to get help quickly to the stricken town.*

How the Land Recovers

Nevertheless, there is little that can stand in the way of the dreadful heat of an eruption. All nature can do is to work on the materials after the eruption is over and they have cooled.

Volcanoes are clearly very dangerous places to be near when they are in full eruption. They destroy plants and animals and leave the landscape devastated. What impact do volcanoes have on the natural world? Are volcanic eruptions as much of a disaster for nature as they are for people?

Rebuilding

The Earth's land area is continually growing thanks to volcanic eruptions. Each eruption brings a little more material to the surface. It also produces many gases including those that living things need.

▼ ▶ *These photographs show how an area devastated by an eruption can recover quickly. The photograph above shows new plants growing vigorously on the mountain six years after the eruption.*

▼ *This diagram shows the stages by which nature recovers the land destroyed by an eruption.*

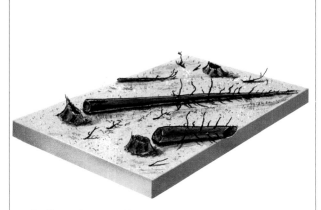

At first the land is barren, with only the remains of dead trees.

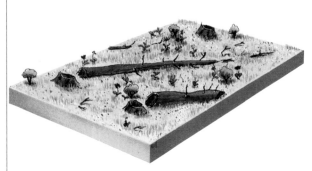

The first seeds blown in on the wind start to grow, others push through from the soil below.

The first plants provide shelter for more plants and the soil begins to be covered again by vegetation.

New life appears

When the eruption has ceased, the ash has settled, and the lava has cooled, the land looks **barren** and desolate. All land on Earth started out this way. To change this harsh rock, where few plants can grow, into fertile soil takes a very long time.

Look among the wreckage of Mount St. Helens and you will already see signs of vegetation bursting through the ash. These plants are called **pioneers** because they are the first to come to this new land. Their seeds have blown in with the wind. The plants have special ways of dealing with harsh environments such as dry soils, midday sun, and winter frost. Some extract food—called **nutrients**—directly from the rock. Some grow by stretching out creeping stems that can form new roots along their length, or by scattering seeds. In this way they gradually **colonize** the volcanic rock and at the same time cover it with newly grown vegetation.

Other plants survive on the edges of the area that has been destroyed. They may have hard scaly buds that only open when they are heated. There may be places where the shoots are protected from the heat. Many plants have buds on their roots just below the surface of the soil. The trunk of a tree may have been snapped off, but that is not always the end. Hidden shoots may soon push through and a new tree starts to grow.

Food for all

The first living things to come back to the site of an eruption are the plants. They are soon followed by insects and other animals. The insects come to feed on the plant pollen, the animals come to eat the insects or the plants. In this way the cycle of life builds and changes. As time passes, and more volcanic rock is broken down, the amount of nutrients builds again. Soon there is a wealth of plant and animal matter to provide food for all.

Why People Die

Probably anyone who lives near a volcano notices its beauty. A volcano may not have erupted for years, so people may think it is unlikely that there will be an eruption in their lifetime. There is, however, always a risk of a volcano erupting. There is also a risk that people may die as a result of a volcanic eruption.

▲ *The farmer who owns the land in this scene may think he is a safe distance from the volcano in the background. Experience shows he is probably still in some danger.*

Lessons from a famous eruption

Probably the most famous volcanic disaster of all time occurred in southern Italy in AD 79 when Mount Vesuvius erupted.

No one believed Vesuvius was still active. There were no records of any eruptions; the cone was eroded and overgrown with vegetation. People had cleared the land and planted vines to make the most of the fertile volcanic soils. Near the foot of Vesuvius two important Roman towns had grown: the business center of Pompeii and the smaller town of Herculanium.

There was some warning that there could be an eruption, but people did not know enough about volcanoes to realize this. From AD 63 there were several strong earthquakes—a sure sign that the land underneath was starting to crack. This

allowed the magma to rise to the surface and reactivate the volcano. Sure enough, without any apparent warning, Vesuvius erupted around noon on August 24, AD 79. Before anyone could rush away from the area, a kind of drizzle had engulfed Herculanium. It was no ordinary rain, but fine pieces of red-hot lava. The nearby town of Pompeii was engulfed in ash and many of its people were buried alive.

Why people may still die

In Pompeii most of the loss of life was caused by ignorance. Today there is no excuse for ignorance, but people still do not believe the warnings of scientists. They like to hold on to their home or their land no matter what the risk. The slopes of Mount Etna in Sicily are still ringed with villages that are growing bigger all the time. People still think a volcanic eruption will not

happen in their lifetime. They are almost certainly wrong! Lava flows destroyed villages on Mount Etna less than a hundred years ago.

Other volcanic disasters

Volcanic eruptions may affect areas many miles away from the volcano itself. Sometimes people living many thousands of miles away may die. Unless there is warning by radio or television these people will not even know disaster is on the way. In 1815, for example, an eruption of a volcano in Indonesia started up a huge ocean wave (called a **tsunami**) that drowned 56,000 people living in coastal towns many hundreds of miles away.

Other effects may take months to develop. In 1783, a huge ash cloud from one of Iceland's many volcanoes covered the land with such a thick layer of ash that all the crops died. As a result the people had no food for the following winter and 10,000 died of starvation—a fifth of the country's population at that time.

◄　*The painting on the left shows an artist's impression of the Vesuvius eruption. It was painted by Joseph Wright in 1774.*

▼　*The area around Vesuvius remains a densely settled area and many people are still at risk.*

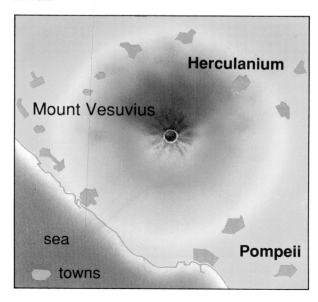

Future disasters

The future disasters from volcanoes will largely be brought about by people rather than by a change in the natural world.

As the world population grows and more and more people try to make a living from the land, the potential for large-scale disaster increases, particularly in **developing countries**. The main disasters will occur in the areas where more and more people live close to volcanoes, like the Pacific. The volcanoes that encircle the Pacific Ocean exist on one of the most active edges of a crustal plate.

Tropical volcanic islands

The people most at risk live on the tropical volcanic islands rather than on the mainland. Often a whole island is made from the tip of just one volcano that rises from the seabed. So when the volcano erupts the people have nowhere to escape.

Tahiti is one such volcanic island in the Pacific Ocean. It is an ideal place for tourism. There are golden sands, warm sea, and a **coral** fringe. The mountain is cloaked in deep green forest. Around the edge of the island there is also flat ground for farming. Tahiti is one of the most attractive places in the world. However, it is certain that the volcano that built this island will erupt in the future. When it does many people on the island may die.

◀ ▼ *Bali, in Southeast Asia, is one of a string of volcanic islands where many people live. The Balinese have farmed the slopes of the volcano for many generations. The neat paddy fields, where rice grows well, represent a life's work. People are not ready to give up such fertile land easily and will accept the risk of an eruption.*

26

The effect of an eruption

When a volcano erupts lava may flow down the valleys and ash may smother the land, but it is more likely that mudflows will rush down the valley floors and out onto the coastal plain. If there are warning signs that the volcano is about to erupt, it will be possible for the people to be evacuated. If there is no warning there will be no time to escape.

Warnings and escape plans

The main problem facing all governments, and especially those of developing countries, is how to give an effective warning and how to organize speedy escape when danger threatens. Many people live in remote places and some do not have

▲ *Tahiti is just the top of an immense undersea volcano. The coral has grown upward from the volcano's submerged flanks and built the flat reef platform that shows as a light blue in the picture. The top of the volcano has been eroded by rivers and covered with thick vegetation. It does not seem to be a dangerous place to live.*

televisions or radios. A news broadcast will probably not be heard by the people who are most at risk. Many roads have not been built for rapid transport and in some places it may be hard to arrange for vehicles to be assembled quickly in times of emergency. Helicopters can only move small numbers of people and they are very expensive. Until these countries have more resources it is difficult to see how they can provide all the help needed in such an emergency.

Great Disasters

During the Earth's history there have been many great volcanic eruptions. Some of them must have been far more spectacular than anything people have witnessed in recent centuries. The highest mountains of North Wales (including Snowdon) are examples of ancient volcanoes that erupted with a force hundreds of times greater than Mount St. Helens. The Scottish capital city of Edinburgh is built on the remains of another violent ancient volcano. The Castle Rock in the center of the city is the remains of lava that once filled the vent of the Edinburgh volcano. Perhaps the biggest eruption of all time was in Queensland, Australia. The volcano erupted with such violence that 1,000 times as much material was ejected as came from Mount St. Helens.

386 sq. mi.

16.25 sq. mi.

1.15 sq. mi.

31 sq. mi.

7 sq. mi.

.4 sq. mi.

| Mount Toba (Indonesia) 6000 BC | Mount Mazama (United States) 4600 BC | Mount Vesuvius (Italy) AD 79 | Mount Tambora (Indonesia) 1815 | Mount Krakatoa (Indonesia) 1883 | Mount St. Helens (United States) 1980 |

◄ *This photograph was taken a few days after the eruption of Mount Pelee on the Caribbean island of Martinique in May 1902. All that is left of the summit of the mountain is a needle-shaped spine of lava. You can see that the main town, St. Pierre, was totally destroyed.*

Disasters that caused the Ice Age

All great eruptions must have caused disastrous changes to the landscapes of the time. Yet even these giant volcanoes may not have been as important as those that erupted about 600,000 years ago. At this time there were several large eruptions in quick succession. The biggest, called Toba, occurred on the island of Sumatra in Indonesia. When Toba exploded it produced a volcanic crater the size of London and all its suburbs. About 240 cubic miles of volcanic dust was thrown high into the air. This was followed by other volcanic eruptions. Each sent large quantities of volcanic dust into the air. The dust may have been enough to block out some of the heat from the sun. In turn this would have changed the climate so that it was much colder on the Earth. This may have triggered the last Ice Age.

◄ *This diagram shows where some of the world's biggest eruptions occurred. All were capable of causing large-scale disasters.*

Historic disasters

Volcanic eruptions have killed large numbers of people in the Mediterranean region of southern Europe. In 1470 BC a huge explosive eruption of the Santorini volcano on the Mediterranean island of Crete, wiped out all of the inhabitants. The AD 79 eruption of Vesuvius in southern Italy, is probably the world's most famous volcanic disaster. About 2,000 people perished. In 1669 the eruption of Mount Etna on the southern Italian island of Sicily killed 20,000 people. This century, by contrast, the biggest disasters have been in Asia and America. The eruption of Mount Pelee on the Caribbean island of Martinique in 1902 was probably the worst in terms of numbers killed. A glowing **avalanche** of fire-hot rock, gas, and ash burst from the side of the volcano without warning. Directly in the path of this glowing avalanche were the 29,000 inhabitants of the town of St. Pierre. The cloud raced toward them at over 125 miles an hour and there was no chance of escape. Virtually everyone was killed. One of the few survivors was a prisoner locked in a basement jail!

Emergency

Volcanic disasters come in many forms. Some, like those where lava flows slowly down the sides of volcanoes, can be relatively easy to deal with. These flows occur over hours, days, or even months. There is plenty of time to think and plan. Others, like the dreadful mudflows of Nevado del Ruiz or the hot gases of Mount St. Helens, are over in minutes. People have no chance to react or to escape. In all cases there will be many people who need help. To be effective, those who come to help in an **emergency** must be knowledgeable about what to do. This means they must understand what kind of disaster they have to cope with.

What really happens

People might imagine that those who are involved in a disaster will panic. This misconception might stem from what you see in many movies. But movies often contain exaggerations of reality for dramatic effect.

During the disaster there usually is little panic. Out of the chaos, a few people naturally take over the role of leaders and help organize others. These people may be good with their hands, they may have some medical skills. They may just know how to "make do and mend." In general a disaster pulls people together so they help each other, even if they are complete strangers.

▼ *Emergency tent hospitals, like the one shown in this picture, need to be set up quickly, ready to treat those who have been hurt without delay.*

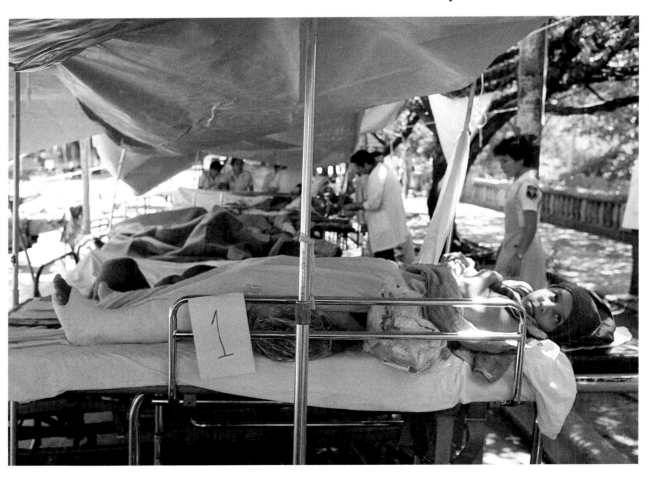

As soon as the worst of the disaster is over people go in search of relatives and friends. The "leaders" and the "teams" break. Some new groups form to help with tasks such as digging people out of the rubble or finding them safe drinking water.

When the rescue teams arrive from outside, the local people may be exhausted. With help at hand some people are happy to let others take control. This will only last for a matter of days. Then the communities will want to be left alone again so they can rebuild their homes and their lives.

Outside aid

People have to act swiftly to provide aid after a disaster. It is thought that the survivors of a disaster need money and help within the first 20-30 days for it to be useful. Even then, the aid from outside will never be more than a small contribution, perhaps a quarter of all costs. The main purpose of outside aid is to tide people over the first few days until they can get themselves organized. The other purpose of outside aid is to provide money to restart factories or help rebuild public buildings such as hospitals and schools.

▲　*Drinking water must be brought to the area because the local supplies may be unsafe. Here water from a tanker is being used to fill the buckets for local people.*

◄　**People who have lost their homes have to gather up what few possessions remain and seek somewhere new to live. These people in Colombia live at high altitudes where it is cold every night. It is vital that they are given shelter immediately.**

▲ *When a volcano begins to erupt, people have to react quickly. Here you see Mount Mayon in the Philippines beginning to erupt. The people in the foreground are desperately trying to gather in their crops before they become buried by ash.*

Emergency for Armero

Earlier in this book we saw how the town of Armero was buried by volcanic mud in a matter of minutes. People did not have time to help each other. As soon as the mudflow wave had passed and there was daylight, rescue teams were able to help.

The armed forces were the first outsiders to arrive because they could get to the area quickly using helicopters. The roads to the town had been washed away and they had to be rebuilt as quickly as possible. This was a job for the army. Those who were injured needed to be carried to hospitals in other towns by helicopter. The Colombian army did not have the resources to act alone, and they soon got help from the United States army. Mexico also sent a medical team to the area just two months after its own disastrous earthquake. The

Mexicans said that because they had suffered in a disaster they knew how others felt. Now they wanted to help the survivors.

The next urgent need was to provide food. A church in a town nearby was used as an emergency warehouse. The priest and others offered to sort out food that had been donated.

In Armero there was no clean drinking water left and there was a risk of disease. Everyone in the area had to be **inoculated** to prevent an outbreak of illness.

Then the survivors had to be housed. A village of tents was erected. It was some weeks before anything could be rebuilt. The main problem was the lack of people. So many had been killed that the town had been reduced to a village. Those who were left did not want to move away. They wanted to rebuild their homes and lives.

Emergency on Heimaey

Almost nothing could be a greater contrast than the disaster in Colombia and the one in Iceland. The Icelandic government knew that an eruption was likely to happen somewhere in their country. It had made plans for the rapid evacuation of people as soon as an eruption began. In Heimaey everyone was out of the danger area within four hours, plenty of time for the sort of eruption expected in Iceland. Workers were able to return to the island to gather up people's belongings. Even while the eruption was at its height, the workers were trying to limit the amount of damage from the volcano. A team of people tried using bulldozers to build a dam of rock to stop the lava flow advancing on the town. Others were up on rooftops scraping away the ash that fell. This prevented most of the roofs from collapsing under the weight of the ash. In the harbor and on land people were trying to bring the lava flow to a halt by spraying water on the end of it. They had some success.

◀ ▼ *Houses stand empty amidst a sea of ash in Heimaey. The houses are not in immediate danger because workmen have cleared the roofs of most of the ash.*

Be Prepared

Volcanoes erupt in many different ways. Those who live in areas with volcanoes have to be prepared for any of the following terrifying experiences: clouds of gas and ash; rivers of molten lava; huge water waves called tsunami that can bring destruction to coastal towns and cities.

How can people be prepared for such a wide variety of effects? How can they avoid the dangers? Knowing what might happen in the case of an eruption, making plans to save themselves and their homes may help to cut down the risks.

Where the risk is high

The Earth's volcanoes occur mostly along the edges of crustal plates. The main areas at risk lie along the boundaries where plates collide. These areas include places where there have not been any active volcanoes recently. The Cascade Mountains (which contain Mount St. Helens) in the northwest are typical of this type of area. All the mountains are volcanoes. They mark the area where the Pacific Ocean plate is pushing under the edge of the North American plate.

However, the risk of disaster in this sparsely populated area is limited compared to the risk in many other parts of the Pacific Ocean. This is because the great volcanoes, such as Mount Fuji in Japan, tower over major cities where tens of millions of people live. The risk throughout densely populated eastern Asia is very high.

The risk from a volcano can be very misleading. Many people think they are safe because they live near a volcano that has not erupted in their lifetime. However, scientists have discovered that the longer the time between eruptions the more explosive the next one will be. So volcanoes that have been **dormant** through human history may not be at all safe. In fact they

▼ *Many of Japan's largest cities are overlooked by towering volcanoes. This is Mount Sakurajima. The city planners have to be prepared for a major eruption.*

may be just the ones to produce very large future disasters! Volcanoes are part of Earth movements that may take many millions of years to complete.

Lessons from the past

One way to be prepared is to look at past eruptions and learn the lessons that they give. People close to an eruption can be in the way of a lava flow or they can be buried by hot ash or killed by boiling gas. This was the lesson of Mount St. Helens. If you are dealing with an explosive type of volcano, don't live too close to it!

People who live on the slopes of a volcano where lava flows usually occur can make sure their homes are not in the path of the flows. Lava trails give a clear guide to the most likely route future lava flows will take.

Preventing disasters

The paths of slow flows of lava can be changed, as the people of Heimaey, Iceland, discovered with relief. Sometimes bulldozers can be used to make dams and block off the flow in one direction. Engineers have also used dynamite to blow a gap in the walls of some lava channels, to change the direction of the lava flow.

People who live in valleys on the sides of volcanoes are in danger from mudflows. One way to prevent another disaster like Armero in Colombia is to encourage people to build their houses higher up the sides of such valleys.

Most of the volcanic islands on the west of the Pacific have active volcanoes overlooking major cities. Many of these cities could be destroyed by mudflows. Ten percent of the world's active volcanoes are to be found in Japan. The Japanese try to prevent destruction by building great dams of steel and concrete. On the valleys leading from the major volcanoes dam after dam is placed in the way of a possible mudflow. The dams trap large boulders and help to slow down the mudflow. The Japanese have also set up special detectors that warn of a mudflow and a network of television cameras all trained on the danger spots. The goal is to buy time for the villages that might be in danger so that they can be evacuated.

Some volcanoes, such as Mount Sakurajima, have erupted over four hundred times in one year! With dangers like that Japan has become the world's leader in mudflow prevention.

▶ **The deep ravines that score the flanks of Japanese volcanoes can easily channel mudflows. By building many check dams in major ravines the Japanese hope to slow down such mudflows.**

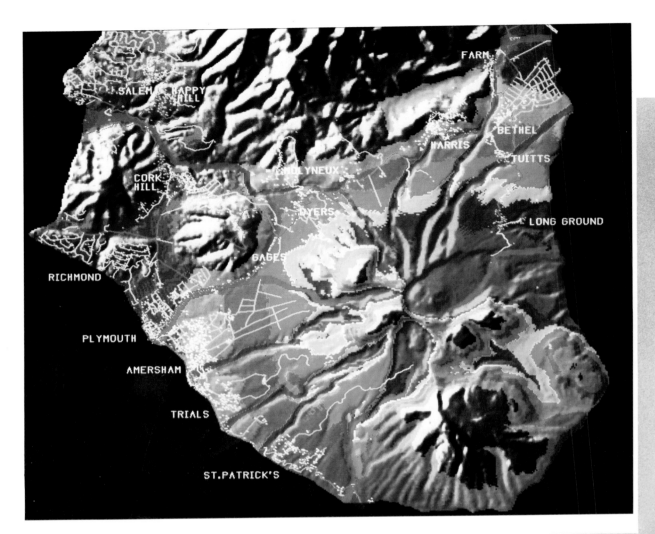

▲   *This computer map shows one way the volcano on a West Indies island, Montserrat, may erupt. The red and purple colored areas will suffer mudflows in the first few hours of the eruption. Then ash will spread more widely, covering larger and larger areas. The blue area will be affected next, then the orange, green, and finally the yellow. Other areas will not be affected. The map shows areas where people need to be evacuated. In the southwest the evacuation should start with St. Patricks, moving people north up the coastal road, then Trials should be evacuated and lastly the town of Amersham.*

   The government can also use these maps to show areas where it is safe to build in the future. Hospitals and control centers, schools, and new roads should all be placed away from the danger spots.

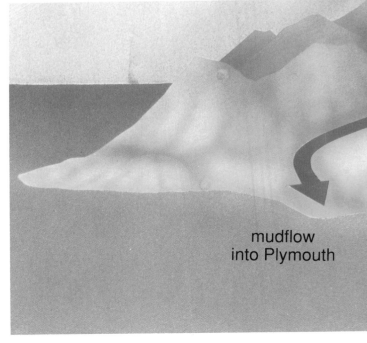

mudflow
into Plymouth

▼ *This is an artist's impression of the part of the island of Montserrat shown on the computer map. It is used to help people interpret the computer map more easily.*

Plan ahead

Scientists now have a much better understanding of the way volcanoes work and they can help predict the nature of an eruption. The latest scientific techniques have been used to help the government of the Caribbean island of Montserrat to make plans in case there should be an eruption in the future.

Montserrat's volcano has lain dormant for 23,000 years, but the hot **springs** on the sides of the mountain show that there is hot magma just beneath the surface. If this volcano erupts again it will probably gather strength over days, weeks, or even months. The first eruptions will be dangerous. Rain-soaked ash will turn to mud and rush down valleys, blocking many roads. Scientists have pinpointed the likely danger spots so that evacuation plans can be prepared taking these spots into account.

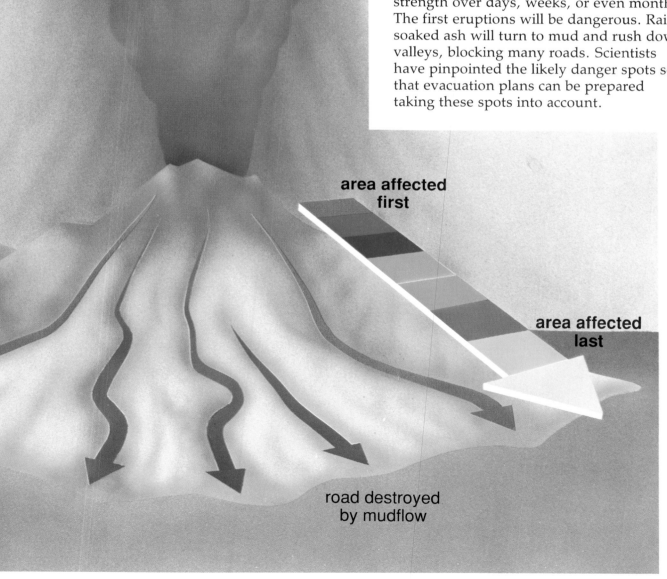

area affected first

area affected last

road destroyed by mudflow

Waiting for Disaster

We have seen how people can try to organize their lives to prevent disaster. However, some people do not use this knowledge. They remain in the danger areas—waiting for disaster.

One country where we can see this happening is Indonesia. It has a population of 165 million, making it the fifth most heavily populated country in the world. Indonesia is made up of a great number of islands that stretch from Australia to the mainland of Asia. All of the islands are formed by volcanoes. On the most densely peopled island, Java, nearly all of the 60 million people live within sight of a volcano. Many people live on the sides of volcanoes.

The reasons people stay

Most people who live in these areas are farmers. For them the chance to grow crops on such fertile soil is a great benefit. As the crusty volcanic rock breaks down, nutrients

---

▼ **Indonesia consists of over 13,000 islands scattered between mainland Asia and Australia. Each island is dominated by a string of volcanoes. This is because Indonesia is in an area where two crustal plates collide. People who live on these islands are in one of the world's most dangerous places.**

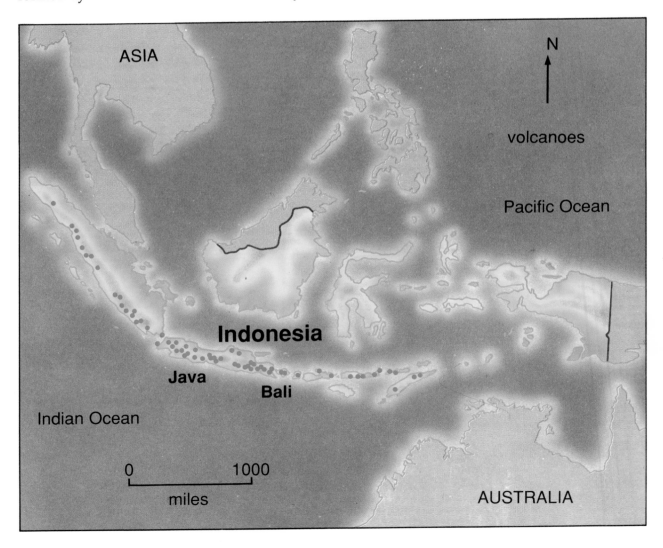

for plants are released. This is like the farmers receiving a free supply of fertilizer. People with little money take the opportunity to make use of these natural sources because fertilizer is so expensive.

The volcanic rocks also soak up water when it rains. The water seeps slowly through the rock and comes to the surface some way from the summit of the volcano. Here it bubbles out in streams all year round. In an area with a long **dry season**, this free and reliable supply of water makes farming easier and more profitable. Good soils, free fertilizer, and free water are benefits that people living in this area feel outweigh the possible dangers from a volcanic eruption.

▶ *These people have worked the land on the slopes of this volcano for generations. They will not move away from the fields of crops they have worked so hard to produce.*

▼ *This photograph shows farmland near the summit of an active volcano. A recent eruption of black lava has buried many fields, leaving only a small ''green island'' of cultivated land.*

Making new fields

Although fertile soil is available to grow crops, people still have the problem of how to farm on the steep volcanic slopes. In Indonesia people make the volcanic soil into steps called **terraces**. They scoop out shallow "trays" across the whole of each terrace. These are then made watertight by stamping on the clay soil. Then streams are

diverted and each terrace is filled to the brim with water to make a special kind of field called **paddy**. Finally rice is planted.

Paddy fields take many generations to prepare, but give some of the most fertile land on earth. They can be used to grow two, and sometimes even three crops a year. They will give a good living to the farmers and provide food for many people.

During the time that farmers have been making paddy fields, most of the volcanoes have not erupted. People hope an eruption will not happen in their lifetime, but the fertile soil is only there because the volcanoes *do* erupt.

◄ *This man values the volcano's advantages more than its risks. The volcanic soils are fertile, while springs from the mountain supply irrigation water. His forefathers have rebuilt the terraces many times after previous eruptions.*

More people to feed

In Indonesia the population is still growing quickly. There is more and more pressure on the land. The government is moving people to less-developed islands to help reduce the problem, but there will always be a great demand for any land. So people farm higher and higher on the slopes of the volcano. The higher they farm the greater the chances that even a small eruption will destroy their fields. This can happen in a matter of seconds and without any warning.

People who live in these places must be prepared to build and rebuild. Their future and prosperity are always at risk.

◄ *This landscape shows the way most Indonesians live—in the shadow of the volcanoes. All Indonesian volcanoes are of the violently explosive type. Anyone as close as this could be in danger.*

▼ *The same scene in 1963 when Mount Agung erupted. This dramatic picture also shows the terraced fields in the foreground. More than 1,500 people are thought to have died.*

Benefits of Volcanoes

How can a volcanic disaster be of any benefit? People clearing up after an eruption would surely not think of a single way. We have seen that volcanic eruptions are nature's way of adding new land. There are other benefits that volcanic eruptions bring to people. Some happen quickly, others take hundreds or thousands of years. Volcanoes can be things of great beauty. Many people benefit from the tourists who come to see the results of a disaster. Volcanoes can also provide sources of energy and minerals, as explained below.

▼   *The remains of Mount Mazama now form the spectacular setting for one of the world's most beautiful lakes. In the middle is the new cone called Wizard Island. In time this may grow to form a new top to the mountain.*

Places of beauty

Mount Rainier, a volcano in the Cascade Mountains, has not erupted for hundreds of years although it is still active geologically. The long dormant period has given time for the summit to be eroded by glaciers. It is now the centerpiece of a National Park in Washington. It attracts thousands of visitors each year. They come to admire the glacier-capped summit, to gaze at the mountain mirrored in clear mountain pools, or to see the variety of unusual plants that grow on the mountainside.

About 5,000 years ago Mount Mazama, a volcano in the Cascade mountain range, exploded so violently that it blew its top right off. What remained was a huge pit. Rain began to fill the pit, and today it has created one of the world's most beautiful lakes. Each year thousands of tourists drive the 25 miles around the rim road of Crater Lake. Wizard Island, in the center, is the tip of the new cone.

Although volcanoes are mostly found on the edges of crustal plates, they are sometimes found many hundreds of miles from the edge. Some of Africa's largest volcanoes are in the center of the continent. Millions of years of activity have formed them into some of the tallest mountains on Earth. Mount Kilimanjaro, on the border between the East African countries of Kenya and Tanzania, rises from a hot dry plain. Kilimanjaro's ice-capped summit is 19,340 feet high.

► *Mount Rainier, Washington, is every bit as dangerous as Mount St. Helens, but between eruptions it attracts many tourists from all over the world.*

▼ *Mount Kilimanjaro is one of Africa's most impressive mountains. This spectacular volcano tells where a new crack in the Earth's crust is opening. The mountain is seen here from over 30 miles away!*

Getting energy from volcanoes

Hot springs, puffing sources of gas, mud pools, and **geysers** all form in areas where there are active volcanoes. Hot springs, mud pools, and geysers are produced as rainwater seeps into volcanic rocks through cracks in the Earth's surface. When the water seeps deep below the surface, it reaches rocks that are still very hot. Here the water becomes heated by the rocks.

As new cold water seeps in, the hot water is pushed out to the surface making hot springs and mud pools. Geysers are

◄ ▼ Tourists come by the tens of thousands to enjoy Yellowstone National Park in Wyoming. They come to see the famous geysers. The most famous is Old Faithful (left) which gushes forth once every 70 minutes. There are many other geysers such as the Castle Geyser shown below.

How many people who visit the area know they are standing on a volcano that may erupt at any moment? The heat that turns the water into steaming geysers could cause an eruption far greater than Mount St. Helens. Scientists know that the Yellowstone volcano has erupted about once every 600,000 years. It might erupt again soon.

formed when the hot water becomes trapped in "dead-end" cracks in the rock. In this case the water is held against the hot rock by the weight of cold water seeping in from above. Eventually the hot water becomes **superheated**. At a critical temperature it turns into steam, throwing a jet of water out of the ground. Geysir, Iceland, has given its name to jets of water formed in this way. They are called geysers.

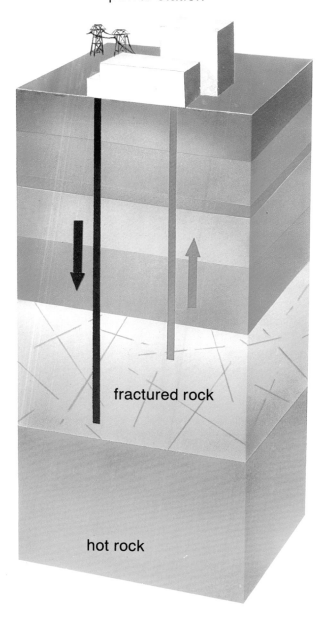

power station

fractured rock

hot rock

People in Reykjavik, the capital of Iceland, make good use of living on a land that has natural geysers. They do not wait for the hot water to reach the surface by natural means. Instead they drill a hole deep into the hot rock, then cold water is pumped down the hole. When the water is hot it is pumped to the surface and used to heat homes and greenhouses, or to make steam which will drive power stations to make electricity.

Minerals for industry

The heat made during volcanic activity causes many metals in the rocks to become liquid. The liquid metals flow up the cracks in the weakened rock and here they cool and solidify. All the world's most famous discoveries of gold, silver, tin, copper, iron, and other minerals were formed in this way.

The people who traveled across the United States to seek their fortunes in the famous Gold Rush to California, in 1849, or the Silver Rush to Nevada in 1859, were digging in the roots of old volcanoes.

People normally only discover the metals buried in the rock when **erosion** strips the volcano away. The many old mines that litter the surface of southwest England show where people dug deep underground near the site of an old volcano in the search for precious metals. Today people high in the Chilean Andes dig for copper in one of the world's most important areas for the valuable metal. The El Teniente mine contains some of the richest ores in the world. The most important export from some countries is metal ore. Bolivia, for example, gets much of its money by selling tin, dug from the roots of its volcanoes.

◄ *Power is gained from volcanic rocks by pumping down cold water. This heats up when it meets the hot rock. The hot water is then pumped back to the surface where it is used to drive the turbines of a power station.*

Glossary

ash
small fragments of magma that are thrown out from a volcano. Ash deposits can be carried many hundreds of miles in a strong wind. Otherwise they fall near the vent of a volcano and help to build the cone.

avalanche
material that falls and bounces down a mountainside. A volcanic avalanche would contain hot ash.

barren
unproductive, bare land. Barren land is normally found near volcanoes that have recently erupted.

colonize
to settle on an unclaimed piece of land. Plants colonize the barren slopes of a volcano after an eruption.

cone
the steeply sloping shape consisting of layers of ash and lava that builds up around the vent of a volcano

convection
the circulating movement within a liquid that carries heat from one area to another. The main circulation in the Earth occurs in the mantle, just below the crust.

coral
a rock material made from the skeletons of vast numbers of small animals. It often forms around volcanic islands as a bank or reef.

core
the center and hottest part inside the Earth. The core is thought to be liquid.

crater
a large pit formed at the top of the volcano vent, usually as a result of the vent exploding

crust
the surface layer of the Earth. It is between 21 and 125 miles thick.

debris
a mass of broken pieces. Volcanic debris often includes wreckage from homes and cars as well as rocks and trees.

developing countries
countries that have not yet become fully industrialized. Most do not have the money to provide a wide range of health, water, and other facilities.

disaster
a severe event that changes the landscape or disrupts the normal lives of people

dormant
a volcano that has not erupted for many years is called dormant. Mount St. Helens was dormant until it exploded in 1980.

dry season
a period of the year when little or no rain is expected. Dry seasons in the tropics last several months each year.

earthquake
a violent shaking of the Earth's surface due to movements of crustal plates

emergency
an unforeseen event that requires immediate action

erosion
the removal of rock and soil from the land surface by natural processes such as running water

eruption
a sudden explosion of material. A volcanic eruption normally begins with large amounts of ash, gas, and steam being suddenly and violently thrown out.

evacuation
an organized movement of people to get them clear of a danger zone

extinct
dead, a volcano which is no longer liable to erupt

fertile soil
a soil that will allow crops to grow well

flood
unusually high flow of water in a river causing the water to spill out of the channel and over areas of the surrounding landscape that are normally dry

floodplain
the flat land on either side of a river channel that is covered with water when a river spills (floods) over its banks

geologist
a scientist who studies the Earth's rocks

geyser
a natural fountain of hot water. Geysers occur where there is hot rock not far below the surface.

Ice Age
a very cold period of the Earth's history. The last Ice Age started about two million years ago and ended about 10,000 years ago.

inoculate
to give a medicine (often by injection). The purpose is to protect people from disease

lahar
a volcanic mudflow. The word comes from Java and describes a mixture of water, volcanic ash, and some gases which moves at high speed down a valley.

landslide
a slide of loose rock and soil down a steep slope

lava
liquid magma that flows from a volcano during an eruption. It is usually orange, red, or yellow in color and has a temperature of over 1,470°F.

lava flow
liquid magma that flows over the Earth's surface

magma
liquid rock produced inside the Earth. When magma flows on the Earth's surface it is called lava.

mantle
the part of the Earth between the surface crust and core

mudflow
a flow of water and debris, that usually looks like brown liquid cement. Heavy rain, melting snow, and ash often mix together during an eruption to produce mudflows.

nutrients
the chemical foodstuffs that plants absorb from rain and soil water. Nutrients are released when many kinds of volcanic rock break down under the effects of the weather.

paddy
a term used to describe growing rice in small fields. Each field is surrounded by small earth walls and flooded with water.

pioneer plants
the first plants to grow in a barren area

plate
a piece of the Earth's crust. Volcanoes and earthquakes occur at the edges of the plates.

pumice
solid lava that has many bubbles of gas trapped in it. It forms as the "froth" on top of molten lava.

radioactive
a substance, such as uranium, naturally releases particles from its atoms. This process can generate heat.

spring
a source of water coming from the ground, enough to start a stream

superheated water
water heated in rocks to a temperature above 212°F

terrace
narrow flat strips made in sloping land to make a place for growing crops

tremor
the vibrations at the ground surface produced by an earthquake

tsunami
sea waves up to 26 feet high that are produced by an earthquake or volcanic eruption below an ocean floor

vegetation
a group term for all plant life that grows in an area

vent
the pipe in a volcano through which lava, gas, and ash escape to the surface

volcanic material
lava, ash, and gases that are brought to the surface when a volcano erupts

volcano
a mountain made from layers of materials that were ejected as molten rock or ash from within the Earth

Index